the Apple and the Egg

the Apple and the Egg

by
Renée
Locks
&
Joseph
McHugh

CELESTIAL ARTS
Millbrae·California

Thank you
Ron Berkowitz
for being a
carrot
in front
of our
nose,
Aaron and Ethan
for sharing space,
Jason and Brody
for being kids,
Jeanette, Carolyn
and
Paula, for their
encouragement
, Nancy,
Tom & John Keel
for being here,
Doug Moran
for

his
presidential
drawing
PBS & WNEW
all the calligraphy
students
for their quotes,
the
universe
for using
us

and all
the consciousness
in or out of the body
that brought
these insights
to
us

Gratefully -
Joe
and
Renee

Why not go out

on a limb?

Isn't that where the fruit is?

pour

away

despair

and
rinse
the
cup
.

Eat happiness like BREAD

EXPECT a miracle

the optimist

fell ten stories.

At each window bar
He shouted to his
friends:
All
right
so
far
.

Unknown

Having read
the inscriptions
upon
the tombstones
of the
great & little
cemeteries
Wang Peng
advised
the Emperor
to kill
all the living
and
resurrect
the
dead

· paul Eldridge

Millions of persons long for immortality who do not know what to do with themselves on a RAINY afternoon.

-Susan Ertz

NEVER
INSULT
an
ALLIGATOR
UNTIL
you've crossed the
river.

Give everyone his Freedom

Everyone includes You!

Be
good
to yourself,
Its the least you can do.
Be good to Yourself
Its the most You can do. I'myro
Be good to yourself. Its the least you can do.
Its the most you can do. Be good to yourself. Its the
most you can do. Be good to yourself. Its the least
you can do. Be good to yourself. Its the most you can
do.

We are no longer
animals,
not yet
gods

Rajneesh

ARGUE for your limitations & sure enough THEY'RE YOURS! *Bach*

It's unlucky to be Superstitious

She
who sleeps
on the road
will lose
either
her hat
or her
head.
-Nizami

You cannot teach a person anything.
You can only help him
to find it for himself

Galileo Galilei (1600)

no
peace
lies
in the future
which
is not
hidden
in this
present
instant

·

Fra Giovanni

the
way
of
the
sage
is
work
without
effort
,
TSH

Yes.
It is better to look
from the window
than not to look at all

but
to look through
the window
cannot be compared

to the

w i n d o w l e s s

s k y

Bhagwan
Shree
Rajneesh

I
will cast
my sorrow
unto the wind
& let it die
in the gleam
of
a thousand
smiling
eyes
!

- Off the side of a van

Lets go out into the sunshine
take off our clothes
dance
&
sing
&
make love
&
get
enlightened

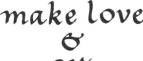

Alicia Laurel

Lightning flashes
Sparks shower
In one blink
of your
eyes you
have
missed
seeing

zen

the Moon
takes up the Wondrous tale,
& nightly to the Listening Earth,
Repeats the story of her Birth.

·Joseph Addison

The important thing is at any moment to sacrifice what we are for what we could become . . .

CHINESE PROVERB

Every single thing
changes & is changing
always in this world
Yet with the same light
the moon goes on shining

—Priest Saigyo

WHEN
FLOWERS
FALL
,
THEY
TURN
TO
DUST
. .
HEED
LESS
'THE
BUTTERFLY
FLUTTERS
AMONG
THEM

.

BISHOP
HENJO

Love your life
Perfect your life
GL☀RY
in your
strength
& beauty
REJOICE
in the
fullness
of your
aliveness

the
GOSPEL
of the RED MAN

YOUR THOUGHTS & YOUR WORDS
My thoughts & my words
BUILD OUR WORLD

Seven Arrows

The poem is not made
of these letters
that I drive in like nails
but of the white
that remains on the paper

Even
the
emperor
cannot
buy
back
One
Single
day

Old Chinese Proverb

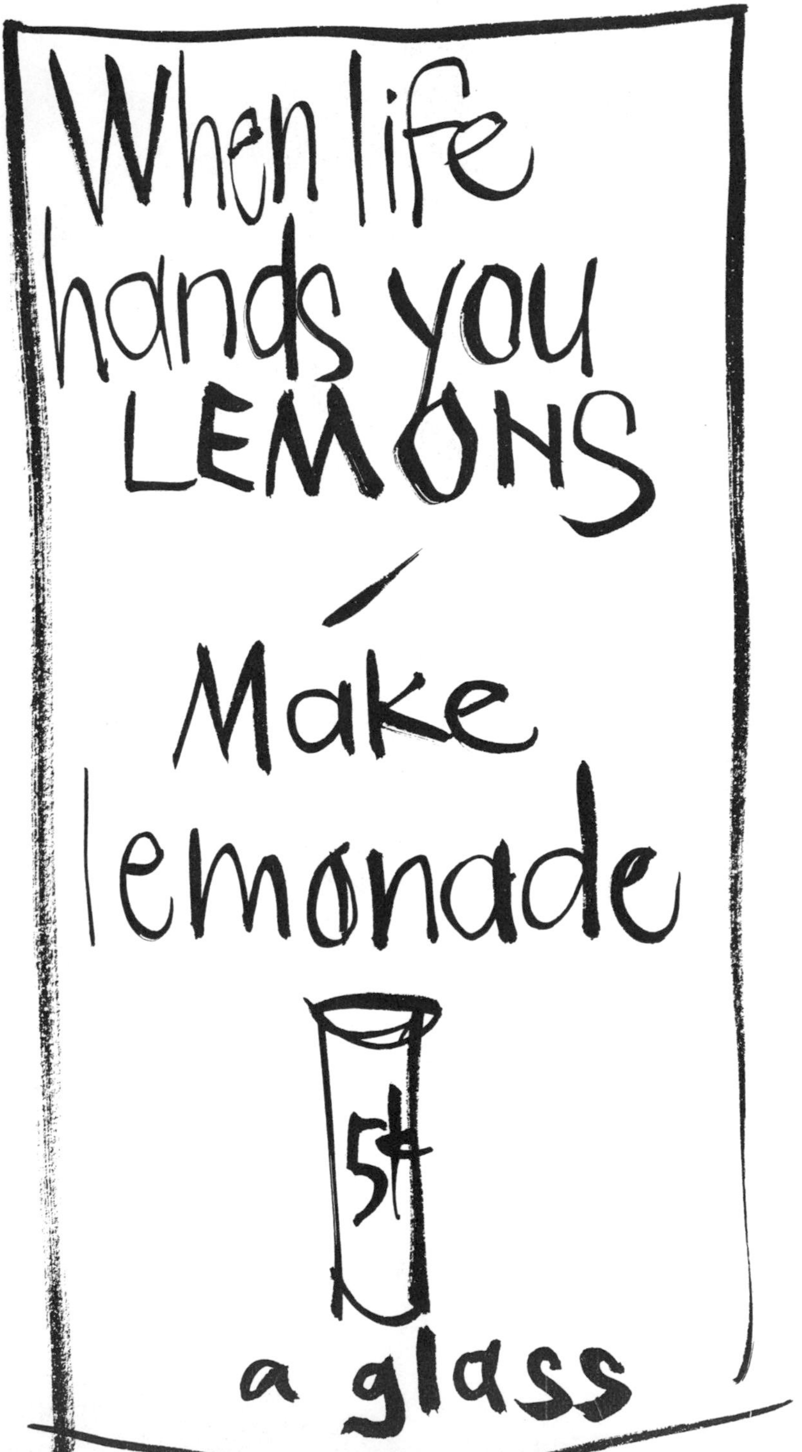
When life
hands you
LEMONS
Make
lemonade
5¢
a glass

If not
you
then
WHO?
IF
not
NOW
then
WHEN
?

—Hillel

the GREATEST SHOW on EARTH

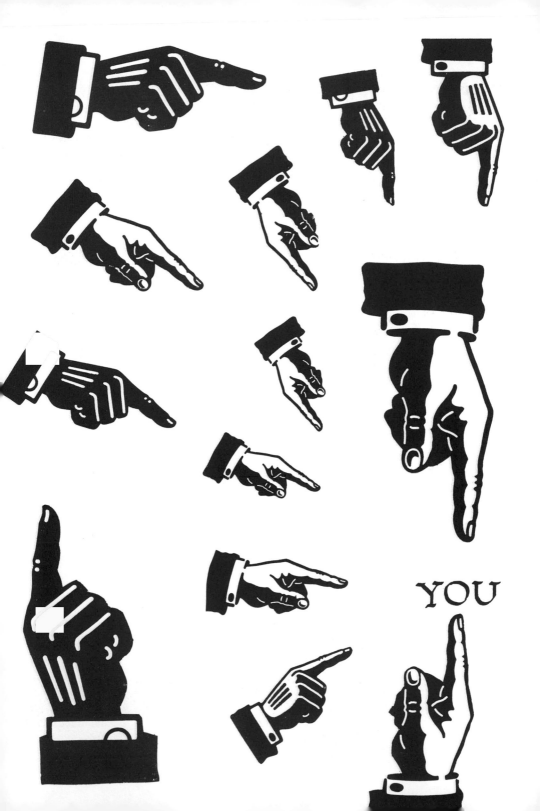

EACH

morning
its like being reborn
. . .

I get another chance
to be
the *Best* me
THAT I CAN BE ·

the Wonder and Beauty and Joy of Each Instant

I DO NOT KNOW WHAT
I MAY APPEAR
TO THE WORLD;
BUT TO MYSELF
I SEEM TO HAVE BEEN
ONLY A CHILD
PLAYING
ON THE SEASHORE
WHILE
THE GREAT
OCEAN OF TRUTH
LAY ALL
UNDISCOVERED
BEFORE
ME

- Sir Isaac Newton

IS STILLNESS

THE GREATEST REVELATION

: : :
&
kisses
are
a
better
fate
than
wisdom

e. e. cummings

the sea has its pearls
the heaven its stars
but my heart
my heart
my heart
has
its
love.

·Heinrich Heine

*I will be the gladdest thing
under the sun
I will touch a hundred flowers
and not pick one.*

Edna St. Vincent Millay

Grant me patience Lord, but hurry

Mary Coffin

A man
is
satisfied
not
by
the
quantity
of
food
but
by the
absence
of
greed

.

Gurdjieff

Desire
is
its
own
discipline

Give me a good digestion , Lord ,
& something to digest .

— Thomas H. B. Webb

We Live & Evolve by "Eating Significance."

Colin Wilson

We
don't
understand
until
we
und*erstand

.Bracha

NOT TWO

EDUCATION
is what remains
after you forget
~everything~

you learned
in school

ALBERT EINSTEIN

Trust in Allah and tie your camel to the post.

Sufi Saying

I
AM
GRATE
FUL
FOR
every
mis
take
I've
made
& noticed
& accepted
& changed

Renée

Each small task
of everyday life
is part of the total harmony
of the universe.

St. Theresa of Lisieux

& God created man
but she
was only
kidding

— Hearsay

Blessed
is he
who
expects
nothing
for he shall not be
disappointed.
—Alexander Pope

YOU CAN COUNT YOUR MONEY
AND BURN IT
WITHIN THE NOD
OF A BUFFALO'S HEAD,
BUT ONLY THE GREAT SPIRIT
CAN COUNT
THE GRAINS
OF SAND
AND THE
BLADES OF GRASS . . .

by a chief of the Northern Blackfeet

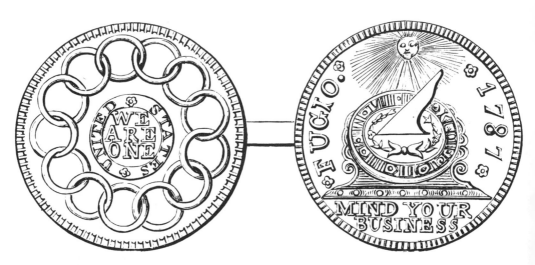

The Franklin Penny — First United States Coin.

I know
    not from theory.
    but from practice,
    that you can live infinitely better
with very little
        money
and alot of spare time
than
with more money
and less time.
                Ezra Pound

I've always
been
crazy
but
its
kept
me
from
going

insane

waylon Jennings

A A A A $ JOKER

IF YOU SIT IN ON A POKER GAME
AND DON'T SEE A SUCKER,
GET UP
YOU'RE THE SUCKER
!

Whispering Saul

he
who
trims
himself
to
suit
everybody
will
soon
whittle
himself
away

No person
for any considerable period
can wear one face to himself,
& another
to the multitude
without finally
getting bewildered
as to which
may be true.

Nathaniel Hawthorne

AVOID

bad memories
negative thoughts
foolish persons

What was it
you were
so
worried
about
a
year

Sometimes
you
never
know
ya
know

A wise old owl
lived in an oak;
The more he saw
the less he spoke;
The less
    he spoke
the more
    he heard:
Why
can't
we all be
like
that
bird
?

Edward H. Richards

A bird does not sing because it has an answer It sings because it has a song

Anglund

The little birds of the field
have God as their caterer.
Cervantes

Flapping
your
arms
can
be
flying

.

Jenna Hall

If you're on the Worry Train
    GET A TRANSFER.
You must not stay there & complain,
    GET A TRANSFER.
The Cheerful Cars are passing through
And there's lots of room for you —
      GET A TRANSFER.

If you are on the Gloomy Line,
    GET A TRANSFER
If you're inclined to fret & pine,
    GET A TRANSFER
Get off the track of doubt & gloom,
Get on the Sunshine Track—
      there's room
    GET A TRANSFER.

If you're on the Grouchy Track,
Just take the Happy Special back,
GET A TRANSFER.
Jump on the train & pull the rope,
That lands you at the station Hope,
GET A TRANSFER.

—Unknown

*Let us knock gently
at each other's heart
Glad of a chance
to look within.*

Carol Haynes

be content
poor heart
life's plans
like lilies
pure
and
white
unfold.

— May Riley Smith

the world of dew ·
    is a world of dew ·
        and yet . . .
            and
                yet

ISSA

The spirit is in yourself,
moving in all things.
-Upanishads

We
shall
be called to account
for
all permitted
Pleasures
we failed
to enjoy.

let me be joy
be hope
let my life sing

Mary C. Davies

I
have
loved
the
stars
too
fondly
to
be
fearful
of
the
night

Sarah Williams

If ever
for a moment
we could pierce
beyond
the
sky

Sarah Williams

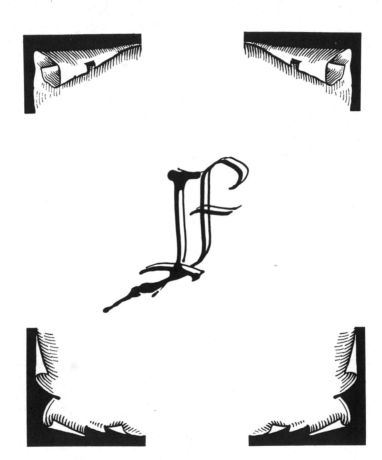

words hang
like wash on the line
blowing
in the winds
of the mind·

- Rameshwar Das

If
you don't believe
in miracles -
you're
not
a realist
these days.
Anwar Sadat

Oftentimes
a little minute
forms
the destiny
of men .
You can
change
the
fate of nations
by the stroke
of one small pen .

· I forgot

there
is
plenty of time
but
each
moment
counts
.
.
.
.
.
.
.
.

THE WORLD SHINES ABOUT ME
LUMINOUS AS THE MOON,
SMILING LIKE A ROSE,
AND A SWEET BENEDICTION
FLOWS THROUGH EVERTHING

·

HOW BEAUTIFUL LIFE IS
I MARVEL AT PEOPLE
WHO ARE NOT
IN LOVE WITH LIFE

·

. . . RUN ABOUT FREELY

YOU ARE BEAUTIFUL
AND YOUR BEAUTY
LIKE THE BEAUTIFUL
THOUGHT OF PEACE
BELONGS TO ALL
ETERNITY

DESSE BARAMA (PEACE)
HAMZA EL DIN
MUSIC OF NUBIA

let your aim be one and single
    let your hearts be joined in one
        the mind at rest in unison
        at peace with all, so may you be
                                    -tao

Love doesn't make the world go round

Love
is
what
makes
the ride
worthwhile

Franklin P. Jones

& IT IS MY FAITH THAT EVERY FLOWER ENJOYS the AIR IT BREATHES

the
BEST WAY
TO MAKE
YOUR *dreams*
COME TRUE
is to
WAKE UP!

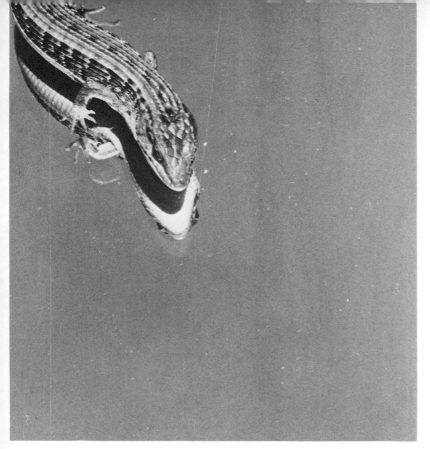

You are not
the
Target

Laura Huxley

Life itself is the thing

Wisdom
is
knowing
what
to
do
next.

If you can't resist
sharing your favorite
adage or quote with us,
mail it to:

the Apple & the Egg
231 Adrian Road
Millbrae, Calif
94030